Dear Parent:

When children are ages 4-6, they learn to use language in social situations, for example, telling a young friend that he or she may borrow a toy or telling another friend that his or her behavior isn't fair. So, reading a story to a child may do more than you think—You are doing your part to encourage future world peace agreements!

Language skills come from practice. Encourage your child to express his or her thoughts. Take time to listen to your child and to answer in clear, simple terms. You will be amazed at how many words your child learns during these formative years. You may find words you use being repeated—so make your own use of language constructive and creative.

We hope you and your child enjoy Sara Raccoon and her friends!

Sincerely,

Fritz J. Luecke

Fritz J. Luecke
Editorial Director
Weekly Reader Book Club

Weekly Reader Children's Book Club Presents

Sara Raccoon and the Secret Place

by Margaret Burdick

A MAPLE FOREST STORY

Little, Brown and Company

Boston Toronto London

For Rachel and Benjamin

Also by Margaret Burdick
Bobby Otter and the Blue Boat

This book is a presentation of Newfield Publications, Inc.
Newfield Publications offers book clubs for children from
preschool through high school. For further information
write to: **Newfield Publications, Inc.**,
4343 Equity Drive, Columbus, Ohio 43228.

Published by arrangement with Little, Brown and Company, (Inc.).
Newfield Publications is a federally registered trademark
of Newfield Publications, Inc. Weekly Reader is a federally
registered trademark of Weekly Reader Corporation.

Library of Congress Cataloging-in-Publication Data
Burdick, Margaret.
    Sara Raccoon and the secret place / by Margaret Burdick.
        p.   cm. — (A Maple Forest story)
    Summary: Away from her noisy brother and sister, Sara Raccoon discovers a
special place all for herself.
    ISBN 0-316-11617-3
    [1. Raccoons—Fiction. 2. Privacy, Right of—Fiction. 3. Friendship—Fiction.]
I. Title. II. Series: Burdick, Margaret.
Maple Forest story.
PZ7.B91624Sar 1992
[E]—dc19   87-26860

Printed in the United States of America

   It was another rainy day in the Maple Forest. Sara Raccoon was trying to sew a dress for Mimi, her monkey doll.

   She was pretending that her bed was a cloud high in the sky, far from the noisy twins.

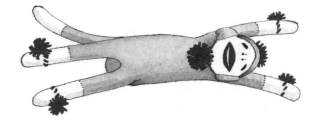

But Frederick said, "I am an owl, and I'm coming to get you! Hoooo, hooo!"

And Erica said, "I'm Erica Eagle, and I'm flying, too! Eeeeek!" And they jumped up and down on Sara's quilt.

"Stop it!" yelled Sara. "Get off! Go away!"

"It's our room, too!" the twins shouted back.

Mother Raccoon came into the bedroom.

"What is all this noise?" she demanded. "Look! It has stopped raining. Everybody outside!"

"Hooray!" hollered the twins.

"Can't I stay inside with you?" asked Sara.

"Not now, dear," said her mother. "I'd like to be alone for a little while. I need some peace and quiet by myself this afternoon. Why don't you play with Bobby Otter?"

So Sara took the twins to Badger's Trading Post to
look for their friends. They collected pinecones along
the way and traded them with Mr. Badger for maple
sugar candies.

"Have you seen my friend Bobby Otter?" Sara
asked Mr. Badger.

"Yes, I have," Mr. Badger told her. "But not since
early this morning, and he said he'd be gone all day."

Sara watched the twins run off with their little friends, the Rabbits.

"Everyone has someplace to be except me," she thought as she trudged along the Silver Stream.

The sky got darker and darker. It started to rain again.

Sara looked for somewhere to keep dry. That's when she found the secret place.

It was in a small tree, too small for a large animal, but just right for Sara. She crawled inside. It was dry and cozy.

"My own special place," she said, and saying it made her feel warm all over.

The next week Sara was very busy. She gathered clover, honeysuckle, and wild strawberries to trade at Mr. Badger's for scraps of calico.

Sara took her sewing kit and made a calico tablecloth. She made calico curtains and pillows stuffed with pine needles. She picked violets and buttercups and put them in a blue vase.

Finally everything was ready.

Humming and churring a happy tune, Sara went
to get Mimi, the monkey doll, for a celebration.

But when she returned to the secret place she had
a dreadful surprise. Someone was inside!

Sara froze. "Who's that?" she called out.

"It's me!" said Bobby Otter.

"How did you get here?" Sara snapped. "This is *my* place. Have you been following me?"

"No," said Bobby. "I was just walking by. I'm going to the sliding hill."

"Well, go then!" Sara said. "This is my secret place. So keep out!"

"You are a Sara Sourpuss!" Bobby said, and he left.

Now Sara did not feel like celebrating. Her secret place was not a secret anymore.

Sara sighed. Why did she have to yell at Bobby? Now Bobby might not let her play with his blue boat. He might call her a Rotten Raccoon. He might say, "Go away!"

Heavy rain clouds began to make the secret place dark. There was no one to talk to and nothing to do. Sara shivered and curled up under the tablecloth. Soon she was asleep.

Thunder woke her.

Oh, what had happened? The secret place was surrounded by water! All the rain had flooded the Silver Stream.

"We have to get out of here," Sara said to Mimi, and she leaped into the cold spring water.

Sara swam and swam, until she came to the
sliding hill.

There was Bobby! He helped her climb up.

"Oh, Bobby!" Sara said. "I am so glad to see you. I'm
sorry I said those mean things to make you go away.
I would invite you back, but now it's too late. My secret
place is ruined." Sara's whiskers trembled and she began
to cry.

"Don't cry," said Bobby. "Your place will be dry again before summer. Meanwhile, we can go to *my* secret place."

"You have a secret place, too?" asked Sara, amazed. "But if I go there, it won't be a secret anymore."

"Sure it will," said Bobby. "It will be *our* secret. A secret is more fun when you share it with a friend."

And it was.